The Wild Bunch
in

The Mystery of the Golden Skate

by
Tony Savageau

Illustrated by
JoAnne Raditz

BLUE MUSTANG
P R E S S

Blue Mustang Press
Boston, Massachusetts

Second Edition
First Blue Mustang Press Edition

This book is a work of fiction. Names, characters, places and incidents are the product of the author's imagination or are used ficticiously. Any resemblance to actual events, locales, or persons, living or dead, is purely coincidental.

ISBN: 978-0-9759737-6-9
PUBLISHED BY BLUE MUSTANG PRESS
www.BlueMustangPress.com
Boston, Massachusetts

Printed in the United States of America

The Mystery of the Golden Skate is dedicated to the real life co-creator of the Wild Bunch, my wife, Karen. Without you, I'd just be a goof. Being <u>your</u> goof makes getting up in the morning something to look forward to each and every day. My love goes to you.

Other books by Tony Savageau:

Wild Bunch Series:
    The Mystery of the Golden Skate
    The Mud House Mystery
    The Sawyer Diamonds Mystery

Travel/Humor Book:
    Train of Thought (with Walter Chalkley)

Acknowledgments

It's been over four years since the first edition of *The Mystery of the Golden Skate* was first published and I'm very excited to see the Blue Mustang Press 2nd edition ready for print. This is the story that launched the Wild Bunch trilogy, and I've stayed true to the original. It's been my honor to visit Massachusetts classrooms and libraries in Mansfield, Foxboro, Franklin, Bridgewater, and Walpole and it's where I have the most fun talking about the Wild Bunch stories and my journey to produce these stories. I wrote the stories hoping my own elementary school children would take an interest in their town and in reading, in general. Now, my youngest is in 5th grade, which is the age most kids have move beyond the Wild Bunch stories as they explore the world books often open up to them. I hope the 'next generation' of kids enjoy the *Golden Skate* story as much as mine did.

Special thanks to my lifelong friend of 27 years, Walter Chalkley for his advice and gentle prodding throughout my foray into books and the publishing game. My wife, Karen, has been a rock of support since this and the subsequent stories were published, I could never have gotten this far without her, nor would I have wanted to. As many already know, the inspiration for the Wild Bunch kids come from my own, Thomas, William and Kelsie. And for *Golden Skate*, there would be no friends of the Wild Bunch if not for Alex, Martha, Joanna, Tina and Eric Rothchild...and finally, thanks to all of the kids who've come up to me time and again and expressed their fondness and have shared alternate plots for this Wild Bunch series. Who knows what the future may bring for the Wild Bunch?

Tony Savageau
Mansfield, Mass.
October 16, 2007

Contents

CHAPTER 1 – Bernie's Cleaners..................................11

CHAPTER 2 – What's That Noise?.............................15

CHAPTER 3 – A Room With a View............................21

CHAPTER 4 – Rose's Discovery................................29

CHAPTER 5 – The Library..35

CHAPTER 6 – The Most Beautiful Skates....................47

CHAPTER 7 – A Calamity..55

CHAPTER 8 – The Fire Escape.................................59

CHAPTER 9 – On The Lookout.................................63

CHAPTER 10 – Gotcha!..73

CHAPTER 11 – Time Is Fleeting...............................79

CHAPTER 12 – The Police......................................83

CHAPTER 13 – Together Again................................89

CHAPTER 14 – Going Home....................................95

Meet The Characters..99

The Mystery of the Golden Skate

CHAPTER 1
Bernie's Cleaners

"Mom, do we have to go with you to that creepy old place? It's the first day of summer vacation and I'd much rather play outside," Joey Wild complained.

"Creepy? You think Bernie's Cleaners is creepy?" Mom replied, shaking her head.

"Yeah, all of the kids at the Jordan School say that place is haunted. People are up there wandering around without heads on the second floor making all kinds of noise," offered little brother Billy.

"You brothers are just plain nuts," an exasperated Rose chimed in.

"Your little sister is right," Mom said, "there is nothing but old washing machines and clothes dryers to be found at Bernie's these days. Now let's get going or we'll never get back in time for dinner! Say goodbye to your dad."

"Goodbye, Dad," the kids replied in unison.

"Have a good time and be sure to keep Rose out of the dryer this time. We couldn't get the static out of her hair for at least three days the last time you were there," Dad chuckled.

"All I can say," Mom replied, "is that I'll be glad when our own dryer is fixed and I can do my two loads a day in the comfort of my own home. Hauling everyone down to Bernie's every other day is getting real old, real fast!"

As the Wild's were driving along Route 106 on their way to Bernie's they talked about the big building that dominated almost half the corner at Main and West Streets. "It's been right there at the corner of Lovell's Block ever since I can remember. That building was built a long time ago," Mom said as she veered left on East Street and passed the school campus. "If I remember my town history correctly, that building was built by Issac Lovell in 1870. Issac's brother, S. Crocker Lovell, was chosen to escort Robert E. Lee through hostile Union lines after Lee's surrender at the Appomattox Court House that ended the Civil War. When he returned to Mansfield, he eventually opened a store in the building his brother built. The building has been home to a general store, a rooming house, even a skating rink some years ago."

This got Joey's attention. "A skating rink? How did they get ice into that old place? I didn't even think they had ice that long ago, Mom."

"Oh, it wasn't an ice skating rink Joey, it was a *roller* skating rink and was a very popular hang out, in its time," Mom replied.

"Roller skating? Here in our little town of Mansfield? That's hard to believe," Billy said. "I wonder when we're going to get that skate park I keep reading about in the paper. Now that is what I'm waiting to see! Roller skating is boring. Skate boarding is cool."

"Billy, you say that only because you can't roller skate!" Rose exclaimed.

"I can too skate," Billy said, "just not very well," he said under his breath.

"Oh yes, the roller rink was quite the social center in its day. Kids and adults of all ages used to go there to skate indoors, mostly on the weekends, right up there on the second floor, as I recall," Mom said with that funny remembering look on her face.

Moms get that look sometimes. Remembering things that go way, way back like they were actually fun or something. Joey wasn't sure about moms sometimes and often wondered how they made it out of their kid years in one piece. He didn't consider roller skating in some creepy old building all that much fun at all. He couldn't even think of anyone he knew who roller skated, unless you count roller blades. And he was fairly certain no adult would ever remember what fun was anymore.

"How does a guy without a head roller skate anyway?" Billy asked as he closed his eyes and tried to imagine what it must be like. He had a hard enough time staying on two feet with his eyes open.

"Billy! Cut it out, there's nobody at Bernie's without a head," Rose insisted, "and if there was, they certainly had better things to do than roller skate."

"Like what?" asked Billy.

"Like looking for their head!" said Rose, "Isn't that what you would be doing instead of roller skating?"

Billy thought about this. Decided it was probably true. And because of that, he didn't say anything to his sister. He didn't like to admit it when she was right.

"OK guys we're here. I've only got two hands so grab a laundry basket and let's set up camp over there in the corner," Mom said.

Camp? This was not Joey's idea of a summer camp. Summer camp involved swimming, baseball, maybe even some artsy stuff, but laundry was definitely not part of the program. Joey thought his mom might be the one going nuts. Still he knew resistance was not an option, so he grabbed a basket, sighed, and headed inside of Bernie's.

CHAPTER 2
What's That Noise?

There was another reason the Wild kids didn't like going to Bernie's and it wasn't just because the building was old and had a funny smell. It was because lately, weird things always seemed to happen when they went off to do things together. Even though Dad was home doing chores before settling in to watch the Red Sox game, today would be no different for the Wilds. Something very strange was about to happen. And that something would get their summer vacation off to a mysterious start.

"Great, let's grab these three machines right here and get started. We've got a lot to do this week and it all begins with this laundry and nice clean clothes," Mom said.

Rose had already stuffed most of her basket's contents into one of the big front loading washers and was waiting impatiently for quarters, tapping her foot and holding her hand out expectantly.

Billy and Joey unloaded their baskets, although with a more deliberate—they would have said thoughtful—Mom would have said slow, pace. Mom added detergent to each washer, gave quarters to each child to deposit into the machines and set them to begin their cycle.

Joey said in his most official voice, "Let the washing begin!" and with a wave of his hand, the washing machines coughed to life.

There was nobody else at the cleaners today, so Mom took out her book, one of her favorites by Janelle Irons. She found a seat near the door and began to read. The kids hadn't thought ahead quite so far and began looking for ways to keep themselves busy until the always-exciting fluff-n-fold stage of the cleaning process.

Joey watched out the side window and looked across the South Common over towards Town Hall. It was a warm summer morning and there were a few people strolling about the Common. Everyone seemed to be in good spirits, and no wonder, they weren't trapped inside Bernie's like Joey. Joey saw his next-door neighbor, Mr. Tebold pushing a stroller with his baby boy, David, enjoying the ride and the sun. He was holding a ball and laughing with his dad as they walked along.

Over there by the bandstand was Mrs. Mankey, Joey's fifth grade teacher, busily making her way towards the café across South Main Street near the Common. Joey liked Mrs. Mankey's class, he learned a lot and felt very prepared for the rigors of Middle School next year. He couldn't believe school had been out for less than a week. Although he missed some of the people in his class, he was very excited to see what the Qualters School had to offer. He'd heard a lot about it and wanted to see how much of it was true. *What a way to spend a day,* he thought. Stuck at Bernie's. What he would give for something else to do.

If only Joey knew what was in store for the Wilds on this fine day, he would have been more careful about what he wished for.

Across the room, Rose had cornered some interesting looking bug and was studying its every move. Not getting too close, mind you, but more than a little interested in what this bug was up to. Rose was very curious in that way and would often stop to analyze the world going on around her. The bug moved very slowly one way, bumped into the wall, stopped turned around and started walking back the way it had come. It was repeating this cycle over and over. There was not much detail that escaped Rose's universe or her sharp memory. The boys were amazed time after time at the things Rose could pluck from the corners of her mind. Whether it was conversations, events years past, or a single 15 second commercial in a week's worth of TV, out of nowhere, Rose would politely remind someone of her recollection. As the boys all too often found out, it was hard to sneak anything by their little sister Rose.

Billy was sitting next to his Mom reading an old issue of *The News* someone had left behind. *The News* was the local paper Billy sometimes read after his Dad was finished reading it at home. As a general rule, Billy loved to read, but he would never admit that to anyone if they asked him. He didn't think his friends would think it was cool that he liked to read. He was really good at spelling and math too. In fact, he liked nothing better than to learn something new about the world around him. And every night you could find Billy in his room reading his favorite book or working on a puzzle before going to sleep. "Hey Joey, get a look at this story. It says right here that this very building we're in right now is going to be torn down soon. Can you believe that? I hope our clothes are dry before then and we're safely at home," Billy fretted, "I don't want to be in here when the plaster starts to fly."

"Bring that over here and let me see," Joey replied. Billy got up with his paper and made his way over to where his brother was standing by the window. "Hmmm, it sure looks like Bernie's isn't long for Lovell's Block. I wonder why they are tearing it down. Sure, it is an old building, but it's been here for such a long time, almost like an old tree. It looks like we've got plenty of time to dry the clothes, Billy. It's not scheduled to come down for a couple of days, best as I can tell from this story. So don't worry." Joey was patting Billy's head. Billy glared up at Joey. He hated pats on the head, but decided to hold his tongue.

While Billy and Joey were looking over the article and commenting about the looming demolition, Billy thought he heard something. "Hey Joey, do you hear that noise?" Billy asked, cocking his head up towards the ceiling.

"What? I don't hear anything except those washing machines," Joey replied pointing over his shoulder.

"Come right over here, stand next to the window, put your hands on the window. Now, tilt your head up just a little, towards the second floor. There. Do you hear the noise now?" Billy persisted.

"Yeah, maybe… I do hear something, but it's not very loud. What could that be?" Joey pondered as he looked around the room for the source. "There's not supposed to be anything upstairs in this building anymore. It isn't safe."

"It sounds to me like something is sliding across the floor or something," Billy said. "Mom said there used to be a skating rink up there. Do you think people are still skating up there?" Billy wondered out loud. "It sounds kind of like the noise we make when we ride our scooters across the kitchen floor...before Mom catches us at least. Or maybe somebody is living up there. Somebody without a head!"

"I really don't think there is a headless body up there, Billy. What have you been reading lately anyway? But Mom did say they used to skate here. Although it was a hundred years ago, just before they invented TV, I think," Joey speculated as he wondered why anyone today would spend their weekends skating on the second floor of an old building like this.

Deciding to see what her brothers were talking about, Rose left her bug and wandered over to them and said, "Hey, what are you boys doing, all whispery and stuff, over here?"

"Go away, Rose. We're trying to figure out something very important," Joey said.

"I'm a good figure-it-outer," Rose insisted. "What are you doing?"

"Do you hear that noise? It sounds like it's coming from upstairs. Except there's not supposed to be anything upstairs," Billy said while moving his eyebrows up and down.

Rose tilted her head. "Sure, I'm not deaf you know,

anyone could hear that," Rose answered sarcastically. "And Billy, what's wrong with your eye brows, are they itchy?"

"What do you think that noise is?" Joey asked her, shaking his head from side to side.

"I don't know. But I know how we can find out," Rose said.

"How?" Joey asked.

"It's simple. Let's go upstairs and take a look around for ourselves." Rose said, quite happy with herself.

"Now why didn't we think of that?!" Billy exclaimed.

"Because you're just boys," Rose replied, rolling her eyes.

CHAPTER 3
A Room With a View

The Wilds began to look around the laundry room, when finally, they found a small door behind some old discarded washing machines in the back of the room. You couldn't see this door from the main room unless you walked back there and really looked. Mom continued reading her book since the clothes were not even on the spin cycle. She knew she had at least 45 minutes to go before they would be ready for the dryers. Her book was getting very good. Mom was not in as much of a hurry as she originally led the kids to believe. She actually enjoyed these semi-quiet times to read for pleasure.

The kids knew they had some time to explore without getting Mom's attention.

"OK, guys I think this door might lead us to the second floor. It's the only other door in this room. Let's give it a try," Joey bravely said.

Slowly, they approached the door and jiggled the doorknob. It was an old doorknob, all rusty and crusty with gunk and grit all over it. Joey jiggled it some more and finally it turned, ever so slowly. With only a little creaking, the door opened. There was a small landing at the foot of stairs with a small high window overhead and to the right. The stairs lead up to the second floor. The kids looked back to make sure Mom hadn't noticed and then stepped inside the landing and quietly closed the door behind them.

"Wow, look at all those stairs. There are more stairs here than we have at home," Billy remarked. And he was right. The stairs looked like they led up to forever. The kids couldn't see where they ended because it got darker and darker the farther up the stairs you looked.

"Yeah, and it looks like the stairs go straight up to the second floor. Can either of you see anything up there?" Joey asked.

"No, it's very dark. I can't see a thing past the first six or seven steps. Maybe this isn't such a good idea Joey," Billy worried. "Who cares what that noise is anyway? Let's turn around and finish up that wash and get home so we can play. What do you say?"

By this time, the boys' imaginations were working very hard. Despite what they wanted to believe, each brother couldn't get the image of an entire family of headless ghouls waiting to devour them as soon as they disappeared into the darkness out of their heads.

All of a sudden, there was a loud CLICK!

The boys jumped at the sound and grabbed each other's arms. Looks of panic spread across their faces. The headless family was making its move towards them; they were convinced of it!

"Let's go boys. Do I have to think of everything?" Rose asked as she flipped a light switch. Heading up the stairs now, "Time is wasting and we've got things to do. So let's get this over with as quickly as possible. Really, let's hop to it."

The boys looked at each other and rolled their eyes. Each thought a similar thought. Rose sure did sound a lot like Mom sometimes.

Joey was not about to let his little sister lead the way up those stairs. He was the oldest Wild after all. So he grabbed Rose's arm, pulled her back gently and said, "Hold on there missy, let me go up first. You will be in the middle and Billy will watch our backs. I can't have you getting into any trouble."

Joey took the lead and headed up the stairs. These stairs were old. At least an inch of dust covered each step. Some of the steps creaked under their weight as they made their way to whatever loomed above. It was obvious nobody had climbed these stairs in a long time.

Rose followed in Joey's footsteps and Billy was right behind his sister. They tentatively made their way past all the cobwebs and dust, and continued up the stairs.

The noise they heard from the laundry room was a little louder here on the stairs, but not by much. Step by step, they made their way towards the second floor. Billy was checking behind them the whole way. He had to be certain someone without a head was not following them. He was not ready to become some headless family's favorite pet boy with a head. So far, so good, he thought and he breathed a little easier.

As soon as Joey got to the top step, the noise stopped, just like that. Almost like someone had flipped another switch. Joey looked behind him to see if Rose was up to her old tricks again. She looked back at him. Joey imagined her saying, *Well, why did you stop?*

Before she could say anything, Joey asked, "Hey, do you hear that?"

"Hear what? I don't hear anything Joey," Billy answered. "Let's get a move on. I don't like these stairs one bit." He looked nervously behind him one more time.

"Exactly! The noise stopped as soon as I got to the top of these stairs," said Joey.

"So, let's take a look around, we've come this far," Rose prodded. "Move on up and let us all into the room why don't you? I want to see what's up here."

As they pushed into the room, they began to look around. The entire floor was a wide-open space. No separate rooms, just a few doors here and there. The four walls were lined with windows. One row of windows looked onto Main Street, one over towards the Common and Town Hall, another towards downtown past Fulton Avenue, and the back wall looked over the old Congregational Church. Some of the windows were boarded up, but many were not. A few were open just a crack, which allowed enough light into the room for the Wilds to be able to see fairly well.

There was a part of the wall with the word "Tickets" stenciled on it and another that read, "Skates". The hard wood floor was almost completely covered in dust except for a small oval that looked like a mini racetrack that circled the room. The kids began to spread into the room to get a better look around.

"Hey Joey, come over here for a minute," whispered Billy.

"What is it? Did you find something?" asked Joey as he turned around to face in his brother's direction.

"Yeah, get over here and take a look at his. You're not going to believe it," a clearly excited Billy replied.

Joey ran over to where he was standing. He was looking out one of the back windows towards the church. Joey's heart was pounding, his mouth was dry, and his hands were all sweaty. He wasn't sure why exactly. He was a little scared to be on the second floor of this creepy building. With some windows boarded up, cobwebs all around and strange noises to boot! Joey knew one thing though. He would never admit he was scared to his little brother and sister. Somehow, his summer had gone from totally boring to almost heart stopping with excitement. Joey reached his brother and crowded in beside him. Billy was looking out one of the back windows.

"Look. Look right there, very closely. Do you see it?" Billy asked.

"What, see what? I don't see anything. All I see is the church over there. I also see where we played outside at recess when we went to pre-school," Joey whispered back.

"Yeah. The playground. Isn't that cool? I never knew how big that church was before this, did you?" Billy asked. "I mean look at the place. It starts over there on West street and goes all the way back to Fulton Avenue. I mean, that church is huge."

Joey's mouth opened but nothing came out at first. He tried again. "You've got to be kidding? You get me all worked up, running over here and that's it? You want me to see where I skinned my knee at pre-school over six years ago? That's it?" Joey hollered in his best holler-whisper.

Billy stared at Joey for a second, perplexed. "I guess so. I thought it was pretty cool," Billy said, smiling. "I mean, look how big…"

"That's it. We're out of here. Let's go. This has been a wild goose chase from the beginning. Let's get back downstairs and prepare to fold like we've never folded clothes before. Mom needs our help; she's only got two hands you know! Jeesh Billy, the playground? You're kidding me," Joey said as he turned to go back down stairs.

Billy, shrugging his shoulders, turned to join him. It was then that Billy noticed Joey hadn't gotten very far. "What's up Joey, I thought you were ready to go?" Billy inquired.

"Billy, do you notice anything strange?" Joey asked.

Billy looked around and thought for a second. "No, nothing strange. It's just you and me, ready to head back downstairs."

That's when Billy paused and realized what Joey was talking about. It was something he hadn't noticed while looking out the window. And even though it was something the boys might have wished for every day of their young lives, they weren't really as happy about it as they thought they would have been. Where they imagined happiness, only dread filled their bellies.

Rose was gone! She was nowhere to be seen. The entire room was empty and as quiet as could be! Rose Wild was missing.

CHAPTER 4
Rose's Discovery

"Rose! What happened to Rose?" Billy shouted in a whisper as visions of headless maniacs snatching his sister filled his head as fast as the 5:25 Commuter train from Boston flew by the Depot each evening.

"I thought you were watching her," Joey said. "She's the little sister, you're the number two son, and it's your job to watch her!" Joey whispered back.

"Me? You're the oldest brother; it's your job to watch both of us. In fact, Mom is gonna be pretty upset you lost Rose. You just better not lose me to the walking, headless dead." Billy said as he grabbed hold of Joey's sleeve.

"We didn't lose anyone. She must have gone back downstairs with Mom, don't you think?" Joey hoped.

"I don't think so, she would have walked right past me and I didn't see her," Billy replied. "And when have you known Rose to do anything without saying something to someone?"

Just then, as the brothers stood holding each other and

wondering how they were going to explain to their parents that their only daughter was now in another dimension, (or worse), a door, on the wall, right behind them, began to creak open, very s-l-o-w-l-y. The boys grabbed each other tighter and turned around, not really anxious to see what was making the noise. As the door opened outward, a large shadow began to move across their field of vision. Joey stood his ground, while still holding onto Billy. Billy closed his eyes tight, sure that a headless ghoul was about to snatch them away like he did their sister. He'd miss his parents. He'd miss his nice room and all his books. And yes, he'd even miss Joey, although he was certain he would admit that to no one.

The door had swung wide open now. There was nothing but darkness beyond the doorway. The boys couldn't see in. They wanted to run, but couldn't. Their feet felt like they weighed fifty pounds each. Everything was moving in slow motion when, suddenly...

"Hey, what's up with the group hug?" Rose asked as she stepped out of the shadows of the closet and into the light. "Look what I found in here behind some old boxes."

The boys relaxed, let out a big sigh and started laughing. "Rose!" they exclaimed together. "What were you doing in there? You scared us both half to death!" Joey said.

"While you boys were walking down memory lane and looking over at the church, I decided I had better have a look around. Otherwise we'd never find out what was making that noise," Rose answered. "So while you guys were hanging out the window, I saw this door and decided to see if it would open. When I opened the door, I realized

it was just a closet and went inside. The door must have shut on its own. Anyway, I was feeling around in the dark when I kicked something. I bent down and felt around with my hands. That's when I found this," she said as she pulled something out from behind her back. Rose was holding a roller skate. It looked to be about a size three. What was funny about that skate was that it was golden in color and looked almost new.

"That's a strange looking roller blade," Billy said.

"It's not a roller blade, silly," Joey responded. "It's an old roller skate! And look at the color. I've never seen a skate that color before. The only colors I've seen before were white or black. And that was in a catalogue from the 1980's."

"Yeah, and look, it's just my size," Rose said. And with that, she slipped on the skate and with one foot pushed off and rolled across the wood floor. She did pretty well, all things considered. When Rose stopped, she turned around to face the brothers. The Wilds just looked at one another.

It was Billy who said what all three were thinking; "Now we know *where* the noise was coming from. It sounded just like the noise Rose made when she pushed off on that skate. But how could a lone roller skate make that noise all by itself?"

"A haunted skate? Maybe. But how could a skate roll around by itself in this old place?" Joey asked "Rose, put that skate back where you found it and let's get back downstairs before Mom misses us. We've got to find out what's up with this place and if the skate is part of the puzzle or not."

Rose took off the skate and tossed it towards the closet door. It landed on its side a few inches from the doorway.

The kids headed back towards the stairs. Joey glanced back at the skate and shook his head. It just didn't make any sense. The sound they all heard earlier was definitely similar to that of the skate rolling across the wooden floor. But no skate could move around on its own, could it? It was impossible Joey thought, as he continued shaking his head from side to side.

When the last Wild disappeared down the stairs. The golden skate made a slight move. Then another, stronger move. On the third try, the skate had righted itself back onto its wheels. The skate began a slow roll across the dusty wooden floor towards the track. Once the skate reached the oval, it began its slow circular journey, around and around the track. Maybe the impossible was possible after all.

CHAPTER 5
The Library

The kids made their way quietly back down the stairs back to the main room. This time, there was no mistaking it, all three heard the now familiar noise as the skate made its lonely journey around and around on the floor above them. But how could that be? What could explain it?

When they turned the corner, they saw Mom talking to her friend, Mrs. Roth.

Mrs. Roth was passing by Bernie's with her children when she saw Mrs. Wild reading her book inside. She stopped to take the opportunity to talk to her friend for a little while.

The Wilds knew what this meant. The Roth kids would be there too. And whenever you had a problem to solve, six heads were better than three. The Roth kids would be able to provide just the kind of help the Wilds needed to help solve this mystery. The Wilds and Roths often remarked how their kids were 'almost-but-not-quite' mirror images of each other.

Hannah was the same age as Joey. Bettina the same age as Billy while Eddie was the same age as Rose. The families had known each other pretty much before any of the kids could actually remember. The families spent time together during holidays, shared a vacation or two on Block Island, and even went to Disney World together during one memorable trip last January.

The kids knew their parents had this kooky plan to have them all get married together, all at the same time, to avoid six separate weddings. The kids often wondered how their parents ever made it this far with that kind of wacky thinking. Didn't they realize getting married was for old people? Sometimes you have to wonder.

"Hey guys, how's it going?" Joey asked. "We've got something we need to tell you, come over here a minute. We're going to need your help too."

The kids walked to a corner of the room and sat in a circle. Joey wanted to make sure the Roths would keep a secret because what he was about to tell them might not be believed by anyone other than those in the circle. Even then, Joey had doubts the Roths would believe their tale.

Joey started at the beginning and quickly related the events of the last twenty minutes to the Roths.

Hannah was a bit skeptical and wanted some kind of proof before getting too far into any Wild scheme.

Joey stood up and beckoned Hannah over to the window. He asked her to place her hand on the window, just as Billy had done with Joey earlier and tilt her head up towards the second floor. "Do you hear that noise?" Joey asked.

"I do hear something," Hannah replied. "You're positive

it's a skate and not something else?"

"Not absolutely positive, Hannah," Joey said. "But trust me on this one, there's something strange going on here and we need to get to the bottom of it. Are you with us?"

Hannah thought for a second. Considered what the rest of her day might be like. She looked at her siblings and nodded with great determination, "We're in this with you all the way Wilds."

Joey and Hannah returned to the larger group where Hannah said, "OK Roths, we've got to help solve this mystery of the golden skate with the Wilds. Let's listen to what Joey has to say."

Joey began, "OK, let's start with what we know. And that's not too much. We know this building housed a skating rink at one time. We know there's a golden skate upstairs. We strongly believe that skate is causing the noise we've been hearing, but we're not really sure. What we don't know is *why* or *how*. That's what we have to find out. Any suggestions?"

"Let's go to the library and see what we can learn about the history of this place," Hannah suggested. "It's only a few minutes walk from here."

"Sounds like a good beginning," Billy said. "My third grade teacher, Ms. Zeedman says if you're looking for information about stuff you don't know, the library is just the place you're gonna find it."

"OK, everyone put their hands in the middle here," Joey said "as a member of this wild bunch, we won't stop until this mystery is solved. Let's go!"

"The Wild Bunch," Billy mused. "I like it."

And so the Wild Bunch was christened at Bernie's on the corner of Main and West Streets. Little did the children know that with this simple act, the rest of their lives would change forever.

Like any good team, the Wild Bunch had a plan; first, they were off to the Town Library to do some research and find out whatever they could about the old skating rink. Maybe, if they were lucky, they might even learn something about the golden skate.

They headed out of Bernie's with promises to their moms they would be back in an hour or so. The moms were still chatting and told the kids to be careful and to be back on time. Even if the clothes were in the dryer by the time they got back, those two would be talking for at least a couple of hours more. Moms were like that sometimes. What the kids couldn't figure out is why the moms seemed so happy to see them heading out the door. You would have thought they would miss the six of them in that little laundry. Oh well, there's just no explaining moms.

The kids skipped out of Bernie's and headed north on Main Street. They walked past the Endless Books bookstore. This was one of Billy and Hannah's favorite stores on all of Main Street. They walked past the bank and the old post office, which now was home to the Elks. Eddie wondered why a bunch of wild animals needed a building downtown when there were so many woods around, but that's a story for another day.

Once they got to the corner, they carefully looked both ways, saw no cars coming, crossed the street and headed up Church Street towards the Library.

"You know what," Hannah remarked, "I think this is the first time I've been down this street without being in some sort of parade." The kids nodded and thought about the times they had been on the parade route for Little League, Brownies, Memorial Day or Boy Scouts. If there was one thing you could count on, it was that your parade would be headed down Church Street at some point during the ceremony.

Continuing their walk down Church, the kids passed some very beautiful, old homes. This area was one of the oldest parts of the Town. The large trees and friendly homes had lots of stories to tell, of that, the kids were sure.

"When's the last time you were at the library?" Eddie asked Rose.

"Not too long ago. My mom and I picked out a couple of books to read just last week. I think they are going to be awesome," said Rose.

"I go once in a while too. Every fall I have to go there to help my Dad pick up the soccer balls and uniforms for his team. It's a lot of fun. I always get a book when we do that," Eddie replied.

Soon, the children reached Hope Street across from Memorial Park. They crossed the street, always being careful to look both ways and headed North towards the Library. Once they reached the Library, the kids went inside and walked up to the front desk.

"Hello children," said Mrs. Reed, the town librarian. "It's so nice to see kids your age interested in reading; especially on this fine summer day. How can I help you?"

"Well," Joey answered, "we're trying to dig up some information about the old building on Lovell's Block downtown. We're most interested in the time when it was a skating rink. We're just not sure what year that was exactly."

"Oh yes," replied Mrs. Reed, "I remember that time well." Then she got that same far off look Mom did in the car earlier that morning.

"Ahhh, Mrs. Reed, the building…history…skating?" asked Bettina.

"Yes, yes of course," replied Mrs. Reed. "Come right this way. Let's find the archives for *The News*. Let me see…that would have been the year…yes, yes, here we go. There are a number of stories relating to the old skating rink. Probably because it was getting ready to close down and many people were interested at the time. Why not start right here with these back issues. Let me know if I can be of any help."

"Sounds great, Mrs. Reed. Thank you very much," said Billy. "We need to split this reading up between the four of us who can actually read. Rose and Eddie, why don't you guys go find some picture books or something until we need you? We'll let you know."

Rose and Eddie looked at each other. "Fine!" said Rose. "You'll need us eventually. And when you do, you better ask nicely."

"Yeah," said Eddie. "We'll go find some picture travel books and find a nice honeymoon spot for the six of us!"

"What?!" said the other kids in unison? It was clear that Rose and Eddie didn't realize the whole mass wedding idea was only for the adults to enjoy.

"Whatever you guys say, just don't wander too far, OK?" pleaded Joey. "We're going to need your help eventually…really. Besides, we can't afford to lose you…again." Joey was thinking back to the feeling in his stomach when he thought Rose was lost. He didn't want to experience that feeling again.

"We won't go too far," replied Eddie. "We'll just be around the corner."

With that settled, Joey, Hannah, Bettina and Billy set about reading through the way-back issues of *The News*. There were a number of stories about big snowfalls, decisions by the town council; even one about the chocolate factory Billy wanted to read more about. He stopped for a moment to think about how even today you could smell the chocolate in the air on warm summer nights. But because it wasn't related to the skating rink, he kept scanning through the papers. After several minutes, Bettina found something she thought might be useful to their search.

"Hey guys, look at this story. It says here that for the final night of skating at the Lovell's Block skating rink, a special night of skating was planned for kids of all ages. There was going to be a skate contest and a number of different prizes. After that final glorious night, the story says, the Rink will be closed forever."

Billy said, "I wonder why they wanted to close the skating rink?"

"It says here because the constant vibration from all of the skating was causing the building to age prematurely.

So rather than fix up the building to handle the vibration, the owner made the difficult decision to shut the rink down," answered Bettina.

"And check this story out," said Hannah, "the day after 'The Last Skate,' a story ran in *The News* about a little girl, seven years old, who won the prize for 'The Most Beautiful Skates' that night. That's nice, but it's not the whole story. The whole story reads that while she was changing back into her street shoes, one of her skates became lost and was never found. The most Beautiful Skates were separated. I wonder if that's the skate Rose found. Although the article here says nothing about its description, we might be on to something. Hmmmm."

"If that is the same skate, maybe it's been skating around in circles all this time trying to find its match!" exclaimed Joey. "But we don't know if that's the same skate. How are we going to find that out?"

"And how in the world will we ever pair them up again?" asked Bettina? "Do we know anything more about the owner of the skate?"

"Boy, it seems like a lost cause. And with the building scheduled to be demolished in just a few days, it's probably hopeless," lamented Billy.

"Maybe not," said Hannah. "The story goes on to say the winner of the contest was the daughter of Mark Heron, who lived on Samoset Avenue at the time."

"But that was so long ago," Joey said. "And where is Samoset Avenue? It sounds familiar but I don't recall where it is."

At that moment, Rose and Eddie came back around the

corner holding some rolled up papers.

"Hey, what are you guys doing?" Rose asked as she and Eddie joined their brothers and sisters.

"We think we're onto something," Joey replied, "but we need to find a map of the town. I'm not really sure where to look and I don't see Mrs. Reed up at the front desk."

Rose and Eddie looked at each other and smiled. "Guess what we have here?" Eddie asked.

"Eddie, we don't have time for games," Bettina replied. "We need to find a map of the town! And we need to find one fast. Time is running out and we have to get back."

"Well, then maybe I've got some good news. As we were checking out places for the honeymoon, we stumbled into the geography section and found this map. Mrs. Reed told us it was a map of town!" exclaimed Eddie. "We wanted you to show us where we lived on this map so we brought it over."

"Great!" Billy said. "Let's see where this Samoset road is located."

Joey and Hannah spread the map out on a table and started to plot different points on the map using bits of paper.

"Ok, Bernie's is here on Main St...right here...the Library is here on Hope Street...over here...we walked up Church St...and...according to the index, Samoset Avenue should be...right here...awesome...Samoset is just a block over from Church street, we practically walked right by it on the way here," Joey said.

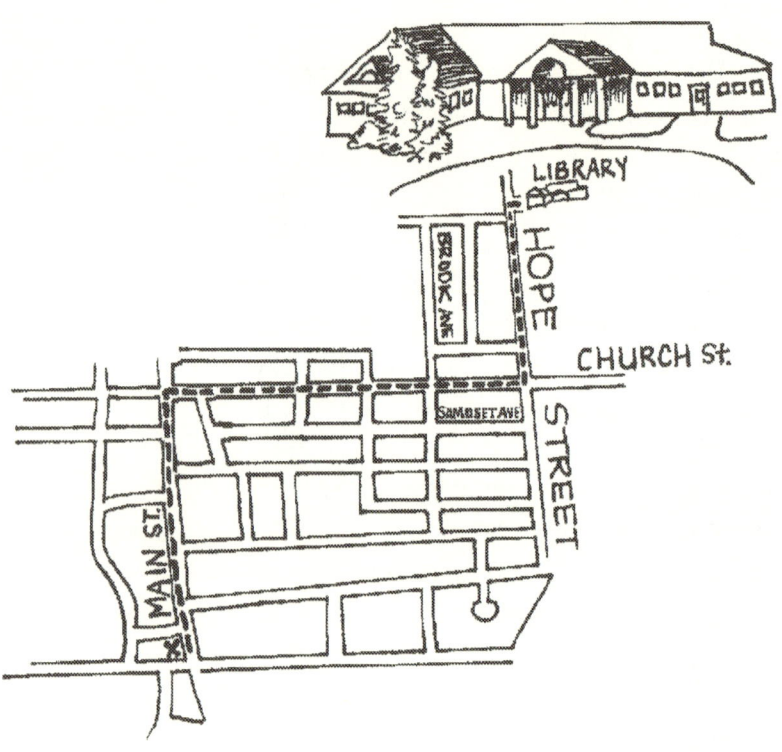

Holding a phone book she got from the front desk, Bettina walked up and announced, "And right here is a listing for an M. Heron on Samoset. What do you think of that?"

"Great work Bettina, do you think it's the same Heron from the story?" asked Billy.

"There's only one way to find out," Hannah replied.

"Call them up on the phone and ask?" Eddie said hopefully.

"Well, yes, so I guess there are two ways to find out. But since we don't have a phone, we're going to have to try the other way. And that means taking a detour on our way back to Bernie's."

"Then let's get going, I'm getting hungry," Rose said.

And the Wild Bunch was off to find the Heron home!

CHAPTER 6
The Most Beautiful Skates

Before leaving the library, the kids stopped at a vending machine in the lobby and used some of the quarters the Wilds had slipped into their pockets earlier to buy some snacks. Mom would have to find another way to pay for the dryers they guessed. Or maybe they'd just have wet clothes to haul back and dry on the line. At any rate, they were all set and ready to go.

They walked out of the library and headed south on Hope Street back to Church Street. They hung a left onto Brook Street until they intersected with Samoset Avenue. They walked down Samoset for a block or two until they came to the address of one M. Heron. The home was a very well kept old cape style. The house was painted white with blue shutters. Joey walked up the path and knocked on the door.

After a few seconds, a tall woman with medium length wavy black hair answered the door.

"May I help you children?" asked the woman.

"Hi. My name is Joey Wild and we're following up on a story we read about in an old newspaper clipping. We were hoping to speak to Mr. Heron."

"A Mr. Heron, you say?" replied the woman. "Well, Mr. Heron no longer lives here."

The kids looked crestfallen. They had hit a dead end. The mystery would remain just that, a mystery. Their exciting summer was over in an hour.

"But, continued the woman, I am Mr. Heron's daughter. My name is Cathie Tolinsky."

"Really?" Joey gushed, "You're the daughter of Mark Heron?"

"I most certainly am," Mrs. Tolinsky replied. "He used to live her until just a few years ago. My married name is Tolinsky."

"Great! "May we talk to you for just a few minutes?" asked Joey.

"Sure, why don't you kids come inside? You might even know my son, Bryan," Cathie said.

"Your son is Bryan Tolinsky?" asked Billy. "Bettina and I know him from school. We used to eat lunch together when were in the second grade."

Cathie replied, "Perfect. You kids look thirsty. Why don't I get us all some lemonade and we can talk."

The children were very grateful for the offer and piled into the living room of Mrs. Tolinsky's home. It was beautifully decorated and very comfortable looking. There was a huge fish tank in one corner of the room with some of the most interesting fish the kids had ever seen.

The kids also couldn't help but notice a number of

pictures around the room with Mrs. Tolinsky as the focal point. She was roller-skating in all of them! In some she was holding trophies or wearing crowns. This had to be the right family connection.

Mrs. Tolinsky returned to the room with a pitcher of freshly squeezed lemonade and enough cups for everyone. Bryan was reminiscing about the good old days of second grade at the Robinson school with Bettina and Billy. They stood in front of the fish tank admiring the fish swimming back and forth and began swapping stories.

For the other kids, it was time to get down to business. And that business was to determine if there was a connection between Mrs. Tolinsky and the golden skate the Wilds had found earlier in the day. Joey related their morning to Mrs. Tolinsky at Bernie's and then spoke about their research at the library. He left out a few of the details that sounded a bit unbelievable even to him, like the golden skate. But he did cover most of the essentials. They had to know if the skate they found was the same skate mentioned in the news story.

"Well you know kids," said Mrs. Tolinsky, "I remember that night very well. I was only seven years old, about the same age as Bryan. I lived with my parents in this very house. My father had come home one evening with a box from Bettie & Will's toy store, down on Main Street. I loved going to that toy store when I had a few extra pennies to spend. Anyway, I opened the box and inside I found the most beautiful pair of roller skates I had ever seen in my life. But what made them really special was their color. They were a beautiful gold color. My dad said they were the only ones like them in the Commonwealth. The wheels were perfectly calibrated, the ball bearings hummed when I spun the wheels and the leather was baby soft. Oh my, I see you've finished your drinks, can I pour you some more lemonade?"

"Yes, please," the kids replied.

"There you go. Now, where was I?" Cathie Tolinsky asked.

"You had just opened the box with the skates inside," reminded Hannah.

Mrs. Tolinsky said, "Yes, that's right. Well the evening I opened that box of skates, happened to also be the last night the skating rink would be open for business. It would be the final night of skating. The next day the rink would be shut down. I had been skating there many times before. But I had never owned my own skates; so I always had to rent my skates from the rink. You were lucky to get skates the same size, never mind the same color when you rented in those days! But that night, I would have my very own, brand new, gold skates. I couldn't wait to get there and begin skating." Mrs. Tolinsky paused for a moment.

"Please, go on," said Bettina who, like the other kids, was riveted by Mrs. Tolinsky's story so far and found herself actually sitting on the edge of her seat.

"My Dad and I went to the rink and went up the back stairs to the second floor. We paid our 25 cents, checked our shoes, and laced up our skates. We began skating around and around. It was a wonderfully cool, summer night for skating. There were not too many people there that night, which was sad considering it was closing night.

But I was able to twirl and spin around the rink without a care in the world. I remember looking out one of the windows that night. I could see the glimmer of the full moon off Fulton's Pond. It was a memorable evening."

"There were a number of contests to mark the closing of the rink. Speed contests, style, pairs, singles, you name it. I wasn't good enough for those contests because of my age at the time, but I knew I had a great chance to win 'The Most Beautiful Skates' prize."

"And did you?" asked Bettina, who already knew the answer, but couldn't wait to hear it from Mrs. Tolinsky anyway.

"Yes. I won. And my prize was a gift certificate for R.L. Steams stationary store. I loved that store too and couldn't wait to use my gift certificate the next day," Mrs. Tolinsky related. "I was on top of the world. Nothing could have made that night any better for me. It was just my dad and me: skating, laughing and having a great time."

"Sadly, however, when my dad and I were changing into our street shoes, along with everyone else, I lost one of my brand new skates in all the hustle and bustle. We looked everywhere, but it was nowhere to be found. I was devastated; those skates were so beautiful. I couldn't imagine what happened to my skate. We checked back a number of times with the owners, but we never found that skate. There was something magical about that night, and something magical about those skates."

"My dad took me to Sweetie's for an ice cream afterwards to try and make me feel better, but it didn't work. I was really sad because I'd lost a skate that my dad had worked so hard to buy me. I loved him more than anything for doing that for me! I decided that night I would do whatever it took to make my dad proud of me. That's when I began to take skating seriously. I saved my allowance and bought a pair of second-hand skates from the owners of the rink. They were a dull brown color, and they were by no means pretty. I practiced every day, out in the street until I was good enough to enter local competitions. I was lucky enough to win a few and earn a scholarship to college because of my skills. But I never forgot those brand new golden skates my Dad brought home to me that night so long ago."

"That's an amazing story, Mrs. Tolinsky," said Bettina.

"Here, let me get you kids some more lemonade; I have more in the kitchen, I'll be right back," Mrs. Tolinsky said.

"Whoa, that was some story," Joey said to the others. "Much better than even the newspaper article."

"Yeah, it's got to be the skate Rose found earlier, don't you think?" asked Hannah. "How many golden skates could there have been that night, at that exact place? I think there can be no doubt about it."

"I agree, it's got to be the missing skate," said Billy.

"Here we are, some more lemonade. I want to show you kids something," said Mrs. Tolinsky. And out of an old square shoebox, Mrs. Tolinsky pulled out a single golden skate that looked almost brand new.

"Is that…?" breathed Hannah.

"Yes, this is the remaining skate from that wonderful night," Mrs. Tolinsky said, "I never got rid of it, I just couldn't bring myself to toss it out. It holds such bittersweet memories for me. I haven't looked at this skate in years. My Dad and I have drifted apart these last few years; we're all just so busy, aren't we? This brings back some great memories."

"Mrs. Tolinsky, thank you for the lemonade and thank you for sharing your story," Joey said, "but we've got to be getting over to Bernie's, our moms are going to wonder what became of us."

Mrs. Tolinsky replied, "It was nice having you all here. It was quite pleasant to share my memories with kids as nice as you. And Bryan would be happy to have Bettina and Billy over to play anytime!"

The kids left Mrs. Tolinsky's house and walked down Samoset Avenue back towards Bernie's.

CHAPTER 7
A Calamity

"We've got to get that golden skate back to Mrs. Tolinsky," said Billy. "It's obvious there is some sort of something causing that skate to try and find her or its match, isn't it?"

"As much as I hate to admit it," Joey replied, "I have to agree with you on this one. Once we get back to Bernie's, we'll run up stairs, grab the skate and return it to Mrs. Tolinsky."

"I think love is making that skate move around," Rose said simply.

Nobody paid her any attention. She was the youngest after all and what did she know?

"Sounds easy enough," Hannah said, "Let's complete the reunion as quickly as we can!"

The kids made their way back to Main Street and were walking up to Bernie's when Bettina noticed something. "Hey, what's that big truck doing out in front of Bernie's?"

On the door of a big dump truck, lettering read

"Calamity Demolition Services – There's Nothing We Can't Wreck." The Wild Bunch knew this might mean trouble for their plan to reunite the golden skates.

Joey went up to the man who was holding a clipboard and looking up at the building. He recognized him as one of the baseball coaches he'd often seen around the Otis Street fields during the season. In fact, as he got a closer look, he saw it was his old T-ball coach and neighbor, Mr. Joditz. "Hey Coach, how's it going?" Joey asked.

Coach Joditz turned around, "Hi Joey. Things are great. How's it going with you? What brings you to town today?"

Joey replied, "My Mom is inside Bernie's washing clothes. We all tagged along and we've been running around town, trying to stay out of trouble. Why are you here today, Coach?"

"Well, we're going to be tearing down this building tomorrow morning, first thing," Coach Joditz replied "and I'm checking to make sure everything is ready and buttoned up for our crew tomorrow. You may not realize it, but your clothes will be the last clothes ever to take a tumble here at Bernie's. After tomorrow, this whole block will be cleared. I guess you didn't see the signs posted around the property?"

"Tomorrow!?" cried Billy, "That can't be, it's too soon!"

"Too soon for what?" wondered Coach Joditz out loud. "The signs have been posted for…"

"We've got to save the ska—rmphfffff!" Rose tried to interrupt but couldn't get it out of her mouth because Eddie had covered it with his hand.

"I'm sorry, what was that?" asked Coach Joditz.

"Oh, nothing Coach," Joey quickly offered. "She does that all the time, it's no big deal. Tomorrow you say? That's pretty fast. We'd better go tell our moms to make sure they've got all our socks out of the dryer, right guys?"

"Ahh yeah, let's go guys," Hannah replied.

"Bye Coach," Joey said with a cheerful wave that hid his true feelings. Joey was worried. They had less time than he thought.

The kids huddled and decided they had no choice but to act fast. As they went back inside Bernie's the moms were still chit chatting away, the wash was in the dryer and spinning like there was no tomorrow. As a matter of fact, there was no tomorrow for Bernie's.

Six kids making their way around the old washers and through the door, all at once, would have seemed a bit strange, even for the chatty moms not to notice. So the kids made a decision to send Joey and Hannah to go up the stairs and grab the skate. It was the youngsters' job to make sure the Moms didn't take notice. Joey and Hannah began making their way to the back of the room while Billy, Bettina, Rose and Eddie got to work on their diversion.

CHAPTER 8
The Fire Escape

The kids fell back on the old standby for grabbing, and keeping, the attention of their parents. They began acting out a favorite of theirs. It was the mock marriage ceremony. Rose and Eddie were the stars. Bettina took her place, as the Minister while Billy took his place as the best boy/flower guy in a scenario that was usually reserved for the annual Christmas night dinner. This was a tradition for the two families that went back many years.

"Dearly beloved, we are gathered here this afternoon to marry Rose and Eddie…" Bettina began solemnly, "…again."

"But I don't want to marry Eddie today," Rose said, I want to marry Smiley."

"Wait, Rose, you'll get a chance to object in a minute," said the ever vigilant Bettina. Bettina was very good at the rules of this particular game. She had been officiating at this ceremony for years, after all.

"Smiley?" Eddie asked, "but he's your fish! You can't

marry your fish, Rose. That's not allowed."

"I know he's my fish, Eddie, and that's because he's my fish. Besides he's cute and he doesn't say much. He's my kind of guy. I want to marry him."

"But you're supposed to marry me," Eddie whispered, "that's what we do every Christmas. How can you marry a fish?"

"Eddie!" Rose whispered back, "in case you didn't notice, it's not Christmas, it's the summer! I only marry you at Christmas. I can't marry you now and at Christmas, that would be wrong!" she reasoned.

"Yeah, I guess you're right," Eddie said. "Bettina, Mom, Mrs. Wild, the wedding is off until Christmas, that's the tradition we've sworn to uphold and we plan to honor it."

The moms glanced up at the kids and resumed their conversation. They were chatting about cabins and a block of islands or something. The kids were not quite clear on that point. But they were sure of one thing; their conversation didn't interest them very much at all.

At about that time, Joey and Hannah came back into the main room and urged the others to join them by the windows facing the Common.

"We've got big, big problems!" Joey said.

"Yeah, we tried to open the door to the stairwell, but it wouldn't budge," Hannah said in an exasperated tone. "Coach Joditz must have locked it to make sure nobody would wander in, when he was doing his checks of the building before the demolition tomorrow. What are we going to do?"

The sound of skate above them was getting louder and

faster. Almost like it sensed the urgency of the moment as much as the kids did.

"We don't have much time," Billy said. "If Calamity tears the building down, the skate will go down with it. That would be a terrible shame!"

"It's too hot in here," Bettina complained, "let's go outside where we can think."

"Good idea," Billy replied, "let's go."

Once outside the kids began to pace up and down the sidewalk. Eddie looked across the street and noticed a bunch of ladders out in front of Paint City on the corner of Main and East Streets. "Too bad those ladders aren't tall enough for us to get to the second floor," Eddie sighed.

"That's it!" Hannah exclaimed.

"What is it?" Bettina inquired, "Those ladders over there aren't tall enough to help anyone get to the second floor."

Nodding his head in agreement, Joey knew just what Hannah was thinking—the fire escape!—"This might work just yet! Let's find the fire escape. Now who's going to give me a boost up once we find it?"

"Not me," laughed Rose, "I don't want to break my back!"

"No, you and Eddie need to be lookouts," Joey said. "Make sure nobody sees us and make sure Coach Joditz doesn't come back either!"

"OK, we can do that, but it's going to cost you a freeze pop when we get home!" Rose chided.

"Deal," Joey said. "Now let's go!"

The kids made their way to the back of the building and found the fire escape near a clothing drop box to climb up on. Billy got down on all fours as Hannah climbed aboard his back and prepared to boost Joey up to the first rung of the fire escape ladder. "OK, ready you guys? On three," Joey said with a little apprehension in his voice.

"One…two…three!" Bettina counted out with gusto as Joey made his way from the drop box to Hannah's boost up to the first rung. He grabbed the first rung and was up the ladder lickety-split.

Joey climbed into the half open window and promptly tumbled to the floor. He found himself where the whole adventure had started about an hour and half before, back on the second floor. Then he noticed something really strange. The sound of the skate didn't stop when he entered the room this time. He sat up facing the window he'd just fallen through. Slowly, he turned around. What he saw almost caused him to jump back out the window, as quick as he could, and head back down to the comfort and safety of his friends and siblings.

CHAPTER 9
On The Lookout

Meanwhile outside, the rest of the Wild Bunch peered up the fire escape and saw Joey's legs disappear inside of the empty window. While Joey was facing the challenge of his young life, the other kids were just about to face theirs.

"Boy, he got up that ladder fast," marveled Billy, "I hope it doesn't take him too long to get the skate and get back down here. Somebody's going to see us back here and wonder what's up."

"Billy, stop fretting like Nana on the highway," Rose replied. "If anyone can get the skate and get back down here, it's Joey. Besides, if he disappears like the skate did, I want his baseball card collection and his room."

"No, I get his room, Rose," said Billy as he was shaking his head. "I'm tired of looking out at the backyard. The woods, the swing set, the…"

"Uh, Billy!…Rose!…Have we forgotten why we're all standing next to a drop box in the parking lot of a building that's going to be demolished first thing tomorrow?" interrupted Hannah. "Let's not forget that we have to return the golden skate to Mrs. Tolinsky. And we're not going to do that if Joey doesn't get down here safely. Now let's spread out and keep an eye out for trouble."

Eddie was tugging on Hannah's sleeve. "But Hannah, if I pull an eye out, I'll only have one good eye to watch out for people. I'm pretty sure the eye I pull out is going to hurt. I'm not sure that is the best plan. I'd like to keep both eyes *in* if it's OK with you", Eddie reasoned.

Hannah stared for a moment at her little brother. There were a lot of things she would have liked to do or say at that moment. None of them would have made her mom or dad very happy. She had to set an example, Hannah reminded herself, and as the oldest kid here, she had to set a positive example. She took a deep breath, let it out slowly, counted to five and replied sweetly, "You're absolutely right, Eddie. Let's use all of our eyes to keep an…I mean to watch out for anybody snooping around. How does that sound? Do you like that plan better?"

"Now that's a plan I really like!" Eddie said, jumping up and down and glad to be keeping both eyes. "What do you want us to do Hannah?"

"Great, gather round everyone and listen to the plan. I read about this in Mr. Marluti's class over at the Jackson school while researching tactics and strategies of great 20th century battles," Hannah excitedly explained.

"Tactics and what of who?" a befuddled Billy wondered.

"Never mind, it's not important," replied Hannah. "What is important is that you listen and listen carefully. We each need to find a spot to be a lookout. We need to agree on the signals we'll use if we see anyone coming our way."

"Like the Wampanoag Indians used to use!" Billy exclaimed proudly, hoping to contribute to the plan. Billy also liked the way Wampanoag sounded and tried to find every opportunity to use it in conversation. Unfortunately, it wasn't very often.

"Exactly. Now, there are five of us so we can have one person on each of the building's corners and one of us will stay here by the drop box to warn Joey if we need to. Are you with me so far?"

All four kids nodded their heads enthusiastically. Each one ready to answer the call and report to duty!

"OK, Rose, you first. I need you to stand right over there at the far right back corner of the building, next to the Food Pantry building. If you see anyone coming your way, I want you to meow like a cat. Got that?" Hannah asked as she pointed towards the back corner of the building.

"Yes, ma'am," Rose replied as she hurried off to her station.

"Eddie, you next. I want you to stand at the far left rear corner of the building facing West Street. If you see anyone coming your way, I want your signal to be a dog's bark. Can you bark?" Hannah inquired.

"Woof, woof," Eddie replied as he scampered off to his post.

"Bettina and Billy. You two are the oldest ones here besides me. I'm going to stay by the drop box so I can help Joey. Or we might need to get him a message in case of trouble. That means I need you to take the two most important lookout spots we have. Are you up for the job kids?" Hannah said in her most motivational tone.

"Send us in Coach! We're ready to play!" exclaimed Billy, who was really getting into this at the moment. Bettina nodded her agreement.

"That's awesome. Billy, I need you to stand at the corner of West and Main Streets. This is the busiest corner we have to watch. It's also the corner we can't afford to let anyone slip by us. Your signal is going to be the sound an owl makes, you know, a hoot, hoot. Off you go," urged Hannah. Billy ran off to find his corner.

"Bettina, you head right up there to that corner of the building facing the Methodist Church. Keep an eye on anyone coming up Main Street or crossing over from Paint City or the church. Your signal is going to be the sound a fish makes."

"Got it! My sound is going to be…the…sound…a…fish…makes? What kind of sound does a fish make?" a bewildered Bettina asked as she moved her lips in a kissy motion, trying her best to make a sound.

Once again, Hannah stared this time at her little sister and thought for a moment. "Actually, Bettina, you make an excellent point. Change of plans. Your signal is going to be the sound a bird makes, a whistle, like our parakeets make at home. Got it?"

"That, I can do!" Bettina said as she jumped up and down and headed for her corner.

As Hannah surveyed her sentries' positions, she saw

everyone was in their place, eyes peeled and ready to give their signals. Hannah climbed back onto the drop box and peered up at the open, empty window. She couldn't hear anything and hadn't seen Joey reappear. "I hope he's OK up there," Hannah half whispered to herself.

Over at her corner, Rose was busily studying some graffiti on the side of the Food Pantry building. This building looked pretty old too. The graffiti looked something like a heart. And in the middle of the heart were letters. Now Rose had just learned to read and began sounding out the words to herself.

Bettina was very alert as she looked up and down Main Street. So far, so good, she thought. Nobody seemed to be out and about the beautiful town of Mansfield at the moment, which she thought was strange. But she also thought it was OK with her. It was a nice day. Where was everyone? She looked up the street and saw Billy. She nodded his direction.

At his normally busy intersection, Billy was thinking the exact same thing as he acknowledged Bettina's nod with a nod of his own. There didn't seem to be very many people outside compared to earlier this morning. Maybe they were all eating lunch he thought. That thought made him hungry. He glanced back through the window into Bernie's and could see his mom and Mrs. Roth laughing and talking. He waved, but they didn't see him.

As he turned around, he saw a car pulling into the gas station across the street. He had always wondered why a gas station had a yellow clamshell for its sign. He knew for a fact there was no seafood being sold at this particular gas station. And even if it did, who would want to eat a yellow clam? In fact, as far as Billy was concerned, who would want to eat any kind of seafood? Nobody in his or her right mind, he figured.

Billy watched as a lady got out of her car and began pumping gas. Billy recognized Mrs. Cooper, a neighbor who lived a few doors down from the Wild family. She pumped her gas, got back into the car and started driving in his direction. She was at the intersection, waiting for the light to change. Billy started to practice his hooting sound, very quietly, just in case. But the car drove right past him down West Street. Billy followed the car with his eyes and gave a little wave to Eddie. Mrs. Cooper was headed his way.

Eddie saw Billy's wave and saw the purple station wagon coming up West Street towards his position. The car slowed to a stop just beyond where Eddie was standing. Eddie could see the Police Station across and just down the street from his spot. Mrs. Cooper got out of the car with a bag of what looked like groceries to Eddie. She began walking up the path to the Food Pantry when she noticed Eddie loitering by the corner.

"Hello little boy, do I know you?" Mrs. Cooper asked, squinting in the sunlight. Eddie mistook the squinty face for a mad face and began to get nervous.

"Maybe. My sister Hannah plays with your daughter Helga sometimes," Eddie answered.

"Oh, yes. I do recall seeing you in the van when your mom drops Hannah off to play. What are you doing standing out here on this street corner? Where's your mother?" Mrs. Cooper asked looking around.

"Well, I'm...pulling my eyes out!" Eddie said proud he didn't let his nervousness get to him. Or so he thought.

"I beg your pardon? Did you say you were...wait, is that Rose Wild down there? I must see what she is up to. What are you children doing out here?" Mrs. Cooper wondered aloud.

And with that, she began to make her way down the side of the building, bag of groceries tucked under her arm, towards the corner Rose was guarding.

As soon as Mrs. Cooper passed Eddie, he began to bark, "Woof, woof, woof!" as he followed Mrs. Cooper down the side of the building. She glanced back at him with a confused look on her face.

When Rose heard the woofing from Eddie, she gave up trying to figure out the words on the building and turned around. Much to her surprise, she saw Mrs. Cooper marching towards her with Eddie only a few steps behind. She wasn't sure what she should do; she started to panic. And so she started to meow in Hannah's direction. "Meow, meow, meow, Hannah...Meee-owwww!" And with that she began running towards Hannah.

Hannah was still thinking about how Joey would get down safely from the window when she heard her brother woofing and Rose meowing. It sounded like a dog and catfight was erupting right around the corner. But when she looked up, she saw Rose running her way, her friend Helga's mom right behind her with Eddie bringing up the rear.

Upon seeing Hannah on the drop box all Mrs. Cooper

could say is, "Hannah, is that...what are you doing up there?"

Hannah jumped down off the drop box to greet Mrs. Cooper. By this time, Billy and Bettina had joined the crowd after hearing all the barking and cat cries from their lookout positions.

"Hi, Mrs. Cooper. How are you doing this beautiful summer day?" Hannah asked with a big smile on her face. "Nice day for a stroll, don't you think?"

With suspicion in her voice, Mrs. Cooper asked, "What are all you kids doing out here? Standing on street corners, playing on drop boxes?"

Eddie knew just what to say, "I told you we were pulling our..."

"Eddie, Eddie, Eddie," Hannah said trying to think quickly on her feet and glancing at the open window above. "There's really no shame in admitting this to a friend like Mrs. Cooper, but, we...we were looking for clothes in the drop box and panhandling on the corner for spare change to feed ourselves!"

Rose began rubbing her tummy. And she meowed.

"What?!" a horrified Mrs. Cooper replied as she looked from child to child. "You poor dears. I just can't believe this. Your families seem so, so well adjusted, but you have no clothes? And you've nothing to eat or drink? It's lucky for you I happened by when I did. I was bringing some food and juice to the Pantry, but clearly, charity starts at home. You kids should have this instead. Here you go, crackers, juice, some peanut butter, take it all. You kids should never have to forage for food like this. And I'll have some hand-me-downs ready for you to take home the next time you come by for a visit."

"Ahh, thank you ma'am," Billy said. "This will certainly hit the spot. We have just one request. Could you please keep this between us for now? I would hate for anyone to find out and get embarrassed, you know?"

"Of course dear, mum's the word. Your secret is safe with me. I just can't believe it. I have to go now. We're having a celebrity telethon on cable to save the bridges over in West Mansfield. It takes so long to get to the Otis Street Fields these days. Something must be done. There's so much to be done and so little time to do it. Enjoy the snacks kids." And with that, Mrs. Cooper headed back to her car, pausing once to look back, sadly shaking her head back and forth.

As soon as she rounded the corner, the kids started laughing and Bettina said, "Clothes...in the drop box...panhandling?"

Hannah laughed, "It was all I could think of. I just didn't want her to look up and see the open window and start asking more questions."

At the mention of the open window, all five kids glanced up and wondered how Joey was doing.

CHAPTER 10
Gotcha!

"I can't believe what I'm seeing! Am I really seeing this?" Joey said in a whisper as he watched the golden skate move slowly in a circle around the room. The skate rolled around and around, with an odd golden glow surrounding it. Joey wasn't sure if it was the sun reflecting off the skate or the skate itself causing the glow. No matter, he still couldn't believe his eyes.

There's no way anybody would ever believe me, Joey thought. He stared at the skate for a few minutes and then remembered why he climbed through the window. He had to get the skate and return it to Mrs. Tolinsky. As Joey walked toward the skate, it began to slow down the closer he got. When he was about three feet away the skate stopped moving altogether. So did Joey.

Looking around the room and feeling a bit foolish, Joey said, "OK, skate, I'm not sure if you can, uh, hear me or not, but I want you to come along with me. We've got someone who might be interested in seeing you." Joey took a step towards the skate. The skate began rolling backwards, away from him. Joey quickened his pace, so did the skate. Finally, he was running, trying to catch the skate as it whirled around the room. Joey wasn't getting any closer. So he jumped at the skate head first, arms out trying to grab it. No luck! He landed hard on the wood floor with a "Whooompff" as the air rushed out of his lungs and dust flew everywhere.

Down below, Mrs. Wild and Mrs. Roth paused their conversation for a second. Mrs. Wild asked, "Did you hear that thump?"

Mrs. Roth listened for a second and said, "No, I didn't hear anything. As I was saying, we had just dropped the dogs at the kennel when Felix gets a phone call from work…" And the two ladies continued talking.

Meanwhile, Joey was lying face down on the floor upstairs covered with dust, trying to catch his breath. The skate had stopped to within 15 feet in front of him and wasn't moving. Joey thought now might be a good time to rethink his plan. So he started thinking. Joey paced back and forth across the floor.

As crazy as it seemed, even to himself, Joey decided the best course of action was to again reason with the skate. He stood up, looked around the room again to confirm nobody was watching. Thinking maybe somebody was playing a big joke on him. Joey was half expecting his brother, sister and friends to jump out from behind a door and start laughing at him. When he was sure nobody was in the room, he began to recount the day's events, aloud.

What a sight to see. Here was Joey Wild having a one-sided conversation with a roller skate! How crazy was that?

Joey went into great detail about the Wild Bunch's visit to Mrs. Tolinsky. Explaining the joy Mrs. Tolinsky felt that night so long ago when she pulled on those skates. The joy suddenly replaced with despair after losing one of her treasures. Then Joey said, "I know I might be saying all this only for my benefit, I don't really know. I think my sister was on to something earlier. I think the love between Cathie Tolinsky and her dad is a big reason you're up here, after so many years. I believe something is causing you to roll around in a circle…searching…for something…each other? I think you've wanted to be found all along. Well, if that's true, I'm here to take you home. Back to Cathie; I think that's what everyone would like to see. But you can't keep rolling away from me. This building will be torn down tomorrow. There will be nothing left in a few days. You'll never get back to Cathie by yourself. I can help you, if you will let me."

Joey was shaking his head and feeling just a little more foolish. Maybe he had it all wrong. Joey looked around again and took a step towards the golden skate. As he moved closer this time, the skate did not move. After several small steps, Joey was standing right over the skate. He bent down to pick up the skate. Hesitating slightly, not sure if he really wanted to go through with this. He swallowed hard and decided he hadn't come this far to run away now. With both hands, he gently picked up the skate.

At the very moment he picked up the skate and stood

up, Joey along with the entire room was bathed in the golden glow. Out of nowhere, Joey heard laughter, music playing; saw lights flashing all around him. The skating sounds of children and adults bounced off the wood floor and walls around him. He saw a man collecting tickets and waving skaters into the room. He saw people sitting on a bench lining the walls as they pulled on their skates. He even heard a girl's voice say, "Daddy, this is the best night of my life, I wish it would never end!"

And then, in less than a second or two, the glow vanished. Joey found himself looking down at the golden skate as he stood in the middle of the room. All the dust, all the cobwebs, everything was back to the way it was when he fell into the room minutes earlier. What just happened? Joey shook his head. Had he day-dreamed the whole thing? He wasn't sure any of what he just experienced had really happened at all. Maybe he was just getting tired. Maybe he was getting too caught up in all the excitement and his imagination was running wild. That must have been it. Or was it?

As he thought about what he'd just witnessed, he suddenly heard giggles and laughter outside of the window he'd tumbled through a few minutes before. Skate in hand, he ran over to the window and looked outside. He saw a woman rounding the corner heading away from Bernie's. He glanced down and saw the rest of the gang looking up at the window right at him. What were they doing now?

CHAPTER 11
Time Is Fleeting

"Are you guys going to help me get down or just stand their laughing and giggling all afternoon?" Joey pleaded.

"Joey!" Hannah exclaimed, relieved to see he was OK. "Did you find the skate?"

Joey lifted the skate up to the window so the others could see it. "You're not going to believe what happened in here," Joey said.

"And you won't believe what just happened out here," Billy answered back.

"Boys! Let's swap stories after we get Joey down and get the skate back to Mrs. Tolinsky," the ever-mindful Bettina said.

"OK, let's get Joey down," Hannah agreed. "Toss the skate to me first." Hannah jumped up onto the drop box and held her hands up towards the window.

Joey carefully held the skate out the window, made sure Hannah was ready and gently dropped it into her hands. "Good catch, Hannah."

Hannah handed the skate off to Rose so she and Billy could help get Joey out of the window safely. Billy jumped up onto the drop box to lend a hand. Joey looked out the window. It seemed to him he was much higher now than when he was looking up at the window from down below. He knew the door to the downstairs wasn't an option. The only way down was the same way he went in. Joey climbed out the window and eased himself over the sill. He let himself hang from the sill. Because Joey was taller than he thought, Billy and Hannah were each able to grab one of his legs as he dangled there.

"Joey, we've got you. Just drop right down, it'll be fine," Hannah encouraged.

"Are you sure?" Joey asked as he tried to get a good look at where he was in relation to the top of the drop box. He felt like he'd been hanging there for hours already.

"Yes, your sneakers are only a few feet from the top of the drop box. Go ahead, you big chicken," Billy taunted, knowing that challenge would entice Joey to drop down and clobber him. Billy wanted Joey to get down from there before somebody saw them and they got in trouble.

"I'm no chicken!" Joey replied as he dropped down to the top of the box. "Now I'm going to show you what it feels like to be pounded by a chicken!"

"Boys, cut it out. I don't think we have time for this now. Look." Rose was pointing towards Bernie's side entrance.

The kids all looked to where Rose was pointing. Heading out the door was Mrs. Wild.

"There you are, kids. What are you all doing over there?

Rose, what's that old thing you have in your hand? Did you get that out of that drop box? You know those clothes are donations. You're not supposed to pull things out of there."

"Ahhh, I didn't Mom," Rose replied. "This skate sort of just dropped in. It's nothing special."

"OK, listen you kids. I'm going to be done with the wash in about 20 minutes. Then we're off. Don't wander too far. When I'm ready to go, we're going. Understand?" asked Mrs. Wild.

"Yes, Mom, we understand. We'll be right out here when you're ready to leave," Joey answered.

Mrs. Wild headed back inside to wrap up her conversation with Mrs. Roth. That 20-minute warning was as much meant for the kids, as it was to give her a "stop the talk" goal. You didn't want to leave any conversation without saying everything that needed to be said. Otherwise, you spent more time later on the telephone catching up on all the things you forgot to say in person. Moms, they are something special, aren't they?

It was Eddie who said, "As you probably know, I can't really tell time yet. But I'm pretty sure 20 minutes isn't a lot of time to get this skate back to Mrs. Tolinsky and get back here in time to leave."

"Eddie is 100% right," Joey said. "We need to move. And we need to move fast. Rose, let me hold onto the skate. Rose handed Joey the skate, it was no time to argue, even though she was thinking about putting the skate on one more time and taking it for a spin. "Thanks. Back to Samoset Avenue! Let's go!"

And with that rallying cry, the Wild Bunch began running back up Main Street on their way to Mrs. Tolinsky's house. It looked like they were on easy street. They were very close to solving the mystery by returning the skate to its rightful owner. They couldn't possibly encounter any more challenges now, right? If you thought, "Right," then you would be wrong.

CHAPTER 12
The Police

The Wild Bunch was making excellent time. They had already carefully crossed Main Street. They cut through the parking lot next to Johnny's Pub and found themselves right on Samoset Avenue. They were about a block down Samoset Avenue when the kids saw a police car approaching them from up the street. The kids slowed down a little bit and waved as the car passed them. As soon as the police car passed them, they began their trot up Samoset. It was then they heard the blast of the police car's siren, "Whooop, whoop". The police car had turned around and was now directly behind them, lights flashing. When the kids heard the siren, their hearts leaped into their throats. The siren really startled them. As soon as they heard the police siren, they stopped and turned around.

Getting out of the police car was Officer Jackson McGerald. Officer McGerald adjusted his nightstick, put his left hand reassuringly on his gun and ambled towards the kids in a slow, deliberate swagger. With a slight

Southern drawl, he said, "Well there young ones. Where do we seem to be headed in such a hurry? Hmmmmm?"

Billy recognized Officer McGerald as his D.A.R.E. sponsor. He felt better now than when he first heard the siren, so he decided to take the initiative and speak on behalf of the group. "Officer McGerald, it's me, Billy Wild, from your D.A.R.E group at the Jordan school."

"What? Who? Oh, Billy Wild. I didn't recognize you. How are you doing? Or should I say, what are you doing?"

"Oh, we're…we're…" Billy hesitated but finally a thought came to him, "out for a jog. Nothing like a little fun run in the early afternoon to get ready for the long haul of summer, right Officer?"

Officer McGerald glanced down towards his shoes. Unfortunately, it had been quite a while since Officer McGerald had jogged anywhere. The only time he could see his shoes these days was after he had taken them off at the end of a long shift. "Absolutely, I know exactly what you mean," Officer McGerald replied. "In fact, I was just thinking about the jog I'm going on later tonight." Officer McGerald was patting his belly as he thought about the several laps he planned to run around the buffet counter at Weng-Mu's Chinese restaurant. As soon as his shift was over for the day, watch out Kung-Pau chicken…you don't stand a chance!

"Then you know exactly what we're up to," Eddie volunteered.

"Of course I do. We received a call about five children begging for food downtown. These kids were apparently bothering the locals and creating all sorts of havoc. I was on my way to check it out when I saw your gang running up the street. A little suspicious, if you ask me. The call wasn't about you kids, was it?"

"Oh, of course not, Officer. As you can plainly see, there are *six* of us. We don't usually beg for food until the big downtown business open house in July," Joey said with a chuckle.

Officer McGerald eyed him carefully. Was he trying to be funny or was he having some fun at Officer McGerald's expense? He took particular interest in the skate Joey was holding.

"I was only kidding," Joey offered meekly. Joey didn't realize Officer McGerald would have been in a much better mood after his planned visit to Weng-Mu's.

"What's that you've got there, son?" Officer McGerald inquired. "Let me see that, please."

Joey's hands started to sweat. There was a ringing in his ears. It seemed as if he was looking at the world around him through a rolled up piece of paper, like a very long tunnel.

"Joey," Rose whispered urgently, "snap out of it!"

"Oh, sorry Officer. Sure, sure, this is a roller skate we always take along with us on our jogs. It motivates us, sort of like a mascot. Here you go," a quickly recovered Joey said as he slowly handed the skate over to Officer McGerald.

"A golden skate," Officer McGerald said almost to himself. "I remember seeing a skate just like this one once before. It was quite a long time ago, before any of you were born. Back when they used to have a skating rink just down the road. Now, what was the story about that skate?" The policeman was tapping his head, holding the skate with one hand, trying very hard to remember. "It seems to me that skate…"

Officer McGerald's thought was interrupted by his police radio, "All Units, all units, a crowd of youths matching earlier descriptions have been reported in the vicinity of the Spring Brook Cemetery. Please respond."

Officer McGerald tossed the skate back to Joey and keyed his microphone, "This is Unit 5. Will respond. I've got to go kids, this could be our mob." Officer McGerald scrambled back to his car. "Billy, don't forget what we learned in D.A.R.E. Y'all be good now. Take care!"

As Officer McGerald ran back to his car, Billy thought that might be as much jogging as his D.A.R.E. sponsor does in a day. "I will, you be careful too!" Billy answered back. The kids were waving after him.

As Officer McGerald turned his car around and set the siren to full automatic, Rose looked over to Joey and said, "Nice going! Your smart mouth almost got us into trouble. Mom is right about that mouth! We almost lost the skate."

"I know, I shouldn't have said anything. I didn't mean any disrespect to the Police. They do a great job around here and we're lucky to have them. But the important thing is, we didn't lose the skate. Now let's get to Mrs. Tolinsky's. We've just lost five precious minutes."

The kids continued their journey to Mrs. Tolinsky's house. There were only a few houses away. Time was running out for the Wild Bunch.

CHAPTER 13
Together Again

Out of breath and nearly exhausted by the excitement of the day. The Wild Bunch stopped in front of Mrs. Tolinsky's house once again. The kids caught their breath and headed up the path to the front door. Joey handed Hannah the skate. Once again, Joey knocked. After a minute, Bryan answered the door.

"Hello, Bryan," Joey began, "we were here about an hour ago talking with your mom. Do you remember us?"

"Sure I do. Hi, Bettina. Hi Billy," Bryan answered.

The kids waved to Bryan.

Joey continued, "I was wondering if we might come in again for just a minute. Would that be OK?"

"Sure, I guess so," Bryan said. "Come in. I'll get my mom."

"Thanks, Bryan," Joey replied.

The kids moved into the Tolinsky's home and again settled onto the couch in the living room. Bryan went to find his mother. After a few minutes of waiting, Bryan returned with his mom in tow.

"Hello kids, what a surprise. I didn't expect to see you all again so soon. It is a nice surprise," Mrs. Tolinsky remarked.

"Hello, Mrs. Tolinsky," Joey began. "We have something else to share with you. When we were here before and told you about the research we were doing at the library about the old skating rink, I left out a couple of things."

"OK, Joey. Please continue," Mrs. Tolinsky said. "You've got my attention now."

"You might want to sit down for this one, Mrs. Tolinsky," Hannah added.

Mrs. Tolinsky looked a bit surprised at that comment. But didn't say anything. She took a seat on the loveseat. Bryan sat beside her.

"Mrs. Tolinsky, when we were here before, I told you we were researching the history behind the big building on Lovell's Block downtown. It's true, we were doing that research, but it wasn't the whole story. I never really told you why we were so interested in that old building," Joey looked to his friends and siblings for encouragement. They nodded and silently urged him to continue.

"We had to do the research because we found something. Something we believe is related to you," Joey said.

"To me? What could that be?" wondered Mrs. Tolinsky.

Joey nodded to Hannah. Hannah brought the skate up from beside the couch so Mrs. Tolinsky could see it. Mrs. Tolinsky looked over to where Hannah was sitting on the couch. She blinked once. She blinked again. Mrs.

Tolinsky's mouth opened, but she couldn't say anything at first. Finally, after looking back and forth between Joey and the skate Mrs. Tolinsky managed to whisper, "Is that what I think it is?"

"Yes! Yes!" the kids shouted. "We think this is your missing skate, Mrs. Tolinsky." Joey confirmed.

Mrs. Tolinsky jumped up off the loveseat and rushed out of the room. The kids all looked at each other with puzzled expressions on their faces. What happened? Had they done something wrong? Was Mrs. Tolinsky too upset? After a few moments, Mrs. Tolinsky returned to the living room with the shoebox she had shown the kids earlier. Everyone knew what was inside that box. Hannah got up and brought the skate over to Mrs. Tolinsky.

Mrs. Tolinsky took the skate, wonder in her eyes, and looked it over. She studied the wheels; she spun them and listened as the ball bearings hummed. She even took in a deep breath to catch the aroma of the leather. "I think this might just be it," Mrs. Tolinsky said. "But I have to be sure." She put the Wild Bunch skate on the floor. Then she opened the box and looked at the other golden skate. She pulled the skate out of the box. Then she picked up the Wild Bunch skate. As soon as she held both skates in her hands, something happened. Joey smiled.

The entire room was bathed in a golden glow. Once again, the sounds of the skating rink came to life. The unmistakable sound of children and their parents laughing, having a joyous time filled the room. And, just as Joey expected, in less than a second or two, the magic was gone. The room returned to normal.

Mrs. Tolinsky looked around the room and said, "Did you kids hear…" the sound of a phone ringing interrupted her thought. "Excuse me one second kids," Mrs. Tolinsky left the room to answer the phone.

"Wow, what was that, Joey? Did anyone else hear that?" Hannah asked.

The kids all nodded in the affirmative. It was Joey who said, "Hannah, I had heard that earlier at Bernie's, just after I captured the skate. It's like a window to the past was opened, just for a second. It sounded like people were having a great time. A very good time."

"I wish I could skate better, it sounded like everyone was really enjoying themselves," Billy said.

Mrs. Tolinsky came back into the room. She was shaking her head. "You are never going to believe who that was on the telephone. It was my dad! He said he read in the paper about the Lovell Block building being torn down and got to thinking about the old skating rink. But because we'd drifted apart these last few years, he had been too embarrassed to call. But today, of all days, he said he had an overwhelming urge to finally make that call. He just couldn't put it off any longer. I told him after all these years I'd finally found my missing golden skate. He couldn't believe it, he sounded so happy. He's accepted an invitation to come by this weekend for dinner. It's going to be so nice to see him. I can't wait until he sees the skates again. We have so much to catch up on."

"The circle is complete," Rose half whispered.

"I'm sorry dear, what did you say?" asked Mrs. Tolinsky, who was smiling from ear to ear.

"Oh, it was nothing," answered Joey for his sister. "We've really got to be going. Our moms are expecting us back any minute."

"That's too bad," said Mrs. Tolinsky. "I can't tell you how thankful I am to you kids. How ever can I repay you?"

"You already have," Hannah replied. "Let's go guys, before Officer McGerald finds us on the missing persons list."

The Tolinsky's walked the Wild Bunch to the door and waved as they ran down the street. "Come back anytime, you're always welcome here." Mrs. Tolinsky called after them. But they were already half way down the street and out of earshot. Mrs. Tolinsky and Bryan went back inside and together marveled at the golden skates.

CHAPTER 14
Going Home

The Wild Bunch ran down Samoset Avenue, cut through Johnny's parking lot, crossed Main and headed back towards Bernie's. By Joey's estimation, they had about three minutes before their deadline. Everyone was feeling really good about how things had turned out. The skate was back in Mrs. Tolinsky's hands. Mrs. Tolinsky and her Dad had reconnected in a way only these kids could really appreciate. Joey decided they had just enough time to stop at Sweeties for an ice cream celebration. Joey dug into his pockets and pulled out a few crumpled bills to pay for everyone's cones. There was no doubt about it; this was the best ice cream in town.

Happily licking their ice creams, the Wild Bunch strolled down Main Street with Bernie's in sight, right down the block. They were laughing and recounting their shared adventure of the day. They were making plans to fill out the rest of the summer. They wondered how they could ever top this day for excitement and fun. That's when they saw their moms waiting in the parking lot.

"Uh oh," said Eddie. "They don't look all that happy."

Joey decided a pre-emptive approach was best and with his best smile said, "Hi, Mom, we're back. And only five minutes late."

"Where have you kids been? Mrs. Roth and I had to carry these laundry baskets out all by ourselves. Never mind, we're ready to go. Say goodbye to the Roths."

The Wilds and the Roths said their goodbyes, with promises to get together again, real soon. The kids took an extra minute to look over Bernie's for what would be the last time. It wasn't such a bad place after all. And now they had their own story to tell their kids someday. The Wilds piled into their mini-van and buckled up for the ride home.

"Coach Joditz came in and told Mrs. Roth and me that Bernie's is going to be torn down tomorrow! Can you believe that?"

Billy said, "You don't say Mom. I hope we get our machine fixed before then."

Mom replied, "Me too. I hope your day wasn't too boring, kids. You all behaved quite well all things considered. We'll try and do something more exciting for you all."

"Well, Mom, I must admit," Joey began, "I wasn't all that thrilled to be going with you to Bernie's today. But you know, we made the best of it. This summer is getting off to a decent start after all."

Joey, Billy and Rose smiled at one another. Yes indeed, this summer was off to quite the start. The kids learned quite a bit about Bernie's and the events that transpired there long ago. Joey couldn't quite believe how things that happened in the past could influence the future, but they did. That's something he would think about for a while. Overall, Joey didn't think they would ever be able to top the fun and excitement they all experienced together today while doing laundry of all things.

If only Joey knew how wrong he was.

THE END

Meet The Characters

Joey Wild is eleven years old and loves to play all sports. But his favorite sport is baseball and his favorite positions are first base and pitcher. Joey was born in Texas and moved to Mansfield when he was very young. He's looking forward to Middle School, but not riding the bus at 7:00 in the morning. As the oldest Wild child, Joey is counted on by his brother and sister to keep a level head and keep them out of jams.

Billy Wild is nine years old and loves to play baseball and go swimming. He enjoys reading and is good at math and science. Billy just finished the third grade where his teacher challenged the class to push beyond their comfort zones and reach new, stupendous heights. He thinks of himself as a secret agent, and enjoys solving mysteries and puzzles using his active imagination and keen sense of humor.

Rose Wild is the youngest of the Wild Bunch at seven, but don't under estimate her. Having two older brothers always keeps her on her toes (which helps her during gymnastics classes too). After this exciting summer, Rose will enter the first grade, which is OK with her because she loves school and learning new things. Always the voice of reason and clarity, you can count on Rose for a perspective her brothers may not have considered.

Hannah Roth is eleven years old and is a soccer stand out in town. She loves to read, write and sing in the school chorus. Always thinking two steps ahead, Hannah loves the challenges kids find in and around the town of Mansfield. If you can't find Hannah on the soccer field, try the town library.

Bettina Roth is nine years old and is regarded by the Wilds as the kindest kid they know. Always mindful of playing fair while playing hard, Bettina enjoys swimming in the ocean as much as she likes family hikes to Mt. Monadnock in New Hampshire. Bettina is also known for taking care of abandoned animals at the animal shelter.

Eddie Roth is seven years old and, like his oldest sister, likes to play soccer. He likes baseball too. A very fast runner, Eddie can be counted on during long hauls around town while looking for fun and adventure with his friends.

Mrs. Wild is the mother of The Wild Bunch who keeps the kids on the move and out of trouble. She enjoys gardening, a clean house and collects baskets by the dozens. Her biggest challenge is finding 'quiet' time in a house full of Wilds. It doesn't happen often, but when it does, Mrs. Wild likes to read or work in her garden.

Mrs. Roth has been friends with the Wilds for more years than any of the kids can remember. Like Mrs. Wild, she spends a fair amount of time keeping the Roth clan busy and challenged in and around town. Mrs. Roth enjoys her annual vacations to Block Island, likes to grow vegetables and cares for the family's six pets, in addition to her husband, Felix, and their three kids.

Mrs. Cooper is a community activist and volunteer who's involvement in Mansfield civic endeavors is legendary. A neighbor of the Wilds, Mrs. Cooper has three children of her own, manages a busy professional schedule, and still finds the energy to give time to the town.

Coach Joditz is employed by Calamity Demolition Services and lives in the Wild's neighborhood. Active as a Little League coach, Joditz can be found at the Otis Street Fields during baseball season where he helps the kids hone their skills. If he's not there, look for him as he drives a large red dump truck from job to job around town.

Officer Jackson McGerald is a very popular Mansfield police officer. Originally from North Carolina, McGerald is a well known D.A.R.E representative for the Jordan and Jackson elementary schools. Most often seen in his patrol car around town, you may also find McGerald at any of Mansfield's popular Chinese restaurants near meal time.

Mrs. Reed is the town's librarian. Most often found in and around the children's reading section, Mrs. Reed is very helpful if you're trying to find just the right book to read at home for you or your kids.

Cathie Tolinsky is the original owner of the Golden Skate and was a champion skater in her youth and lifelong resident of Mansfield. Tolinsky is a fixture at the Robinson Elementary school where she helps teachers and children learn about themselves and the world around them.

Bryan Tolinsky is the nine year old son of Cathie and friends with Bettina and Eddie since the second grade. Bryan is a karate black belt and his favorite sports are basketball and soccer. Bryan is very proud of his mom for all that they've been through together and was very happy to see the Golden Skate mystery solved.

Kids, if you missed the continuing adventures of the Wild Bunch in The Mud House Mystery and The Sawyer Diamonds Mystery, it's not too late to get your own copy! Share in the fun as the Wild Bunch experiences the most exciting summer of adventure in their little town of Mansfield. Be sure to pick up the second and third Wild Bunch Adventures at your favorite local bookstore or online.

EVERY DAY
BUT SUNDAY

THE ROMANTIC AGE
OF NEW ENGLAND INDUSTRY

by JENNIE F. COPELAND

Mansfield Historical Society Edition

LEARN MORE ABOUT MANSFIELD

Today's Mansfield residents have become accustomed to living in a typically modern and active suburb at the dawn of the 21st century. However, Jennie Copeland's *Every Day But Sunday* takes the reader back to a different era in Mansfield. Originally published in 1936, this local classic provides a look at "Our Town" as it was in the industrial age of the 19th century.

Today's reader will feel the affection that Jennie Copeland had for ther hometown of Mansfield, Massachusetts. Now in its fourth printing, *Every Day But Sunday* remains a romantic and enjoyable portrait of the small industrial town that Mansfield once was.

It is with great pleasure that the Mansfield Historical Society and Blue Mustang Press present this fourth edition printing of *Every Day But Sunday.*

ASK FOR IT AT YOUR LOCAL BOOKSELLER OR ORDER IT FROM YOUR FAVORITE ONLINE BOOKSTORE.

Lightning Source LLC
Chambersburg PA
CBHW020413150626
46554CB00013B/836

*9 780975 973769 *